Terence Blacker writes fiction for both children
and adults. The best-sell
first published in 1989 a
into 15 languages so far
children include *The Tr*
Homebird and the *Hotshots* series. When he is not
writing the likes to play the guitar, write songs
and score goals for his footb

What the reviewers have said about *Ms Wiz*:

"Hilarious and hysterical"
Susan Hill, *Sunday Times*

"Terence Blacker has created a splendid character
in the magical Ms Wiz. Enormous fun"
The Scotsman

"Sparkling zany humour . . . brilliantly funny"
Children's Books of the Year

Other Ms Wiz 3-books-in-one titles

Ms Wiz Magic
The Extraordinary Adventures of Ms Wiz
The Crazy World of Ms Wiz

Ms Wiz, Supermodel

Ms Wiz Goes to Hollywood

Ms Wiz – Millionaire

Terence Blacker
Illustrated by Tony Ross

MACMILLAN CHILDREN'S BOOKS

Ms Wiz, Supermodel
First published 1997 by Macmillan Children's Books
This edition published 1998 by Macmillan Children's Books
Ms Wiz Goes to Hollywood
First published 2000 by Macmillan Children's Books
Ms Wiz – Millionaire
First published 2001 by Macmillan Children's Books

This omnibus edition published 2004 by Macmillan Children's Books
a division of Macmillan Publishers Limited
20 New Wharf Road, London N1 9RR
Basingstoke and Oxford
www.panmacmillan.com

Associated companies throughout the world

ISBN 0 330 43406 3

Text copyright © Terence Blacker 1997, 2000, 2001
Illustrations copyright © Tony Ross 1997, 2000, 2001

The right of Terence Blacker and Tony Ross to be identified as the
author of this work has been asserted by him in accordance
with the Copyright, Designs and Patents Act 1988.

1 3 5 7 9 8 6 4 2

A CIP catalogue record for this book is available from
the British Library.

Typeset by Intype Libra Ltd
Printed and bound in Great Britain by Mackays of Chatham plc, Kent

Ms Wiz,
Supermodel

CHAPTER ONE

A Couple of Hedgehogs in a Gale

Although she loved her parents very much, Katrina O'Brien had recently begun to realize that, in certain ways, her mum and dad were really rather strange.

For example, while most parents like a bit of tidiness around the place, Mr and Mrs O'Brien were obsessed with it. Their house wasn't so much a home as a museum where everything was neat, folded and dust-free, pets were banned and friends rarely visited for fear of being told not to make a mess.

"Don't drip on the bath mat," Mrs O'Brien would shout when Katrina was cleaning her teeth in the morning.

"Take your shoes off at the door,"

Mr O'Brien would call out when she returned from school.

"Goodnight, sleep tight – and don't make too many creases in the duvet," Mrs O'Brien would say when she went to bed.

But there was one thing Mr and Mrs O'Brien liked more than tidiness, and that was money. Even though they were quite well off, they were always looking out for new ways of getting rich.

So there was much excitement in the O'Brien house when a brightly coloured card fell through the letter box one evening. Mr O'Brien picked it up very carefully to avoid catching any germs and took it through to the sitting room where Katrina was reading a book and Mrs O'Brien was polishing the chair-legs. With a rare touch of colour on his cheeks, he read from the card.

MODELLING AUDITIONS
World-famous Fashion Designer
Yves de Chiqueville
is looking for well classy models,
aged 8 and upwards,
to model his new Collections
for a Charity Fashion Extravaganza.
Auditions: St James Church Hall,
11 am, Saturday

"Well classy models?" Mrs O'Brien stopped polishing, stood up and took the card from her husband. "Are you thinking what I'm thinking?"

"I think I might be thinking what you might be thinking," he said. "I've read in a magazine that models can earn hundreds of pounds every day. We could be talking . . . serious money."

Katrina looked up from her book. Her parents were smiling at her as if suddenly she wasn't so much a daughter as a winning lottery ticket.

"Well classy model," said Mrs
O'Brien.

"Serious money," said Mr O'Brien.

Katrina shook her head firmly.
"Everyone at St Barnabas has received
these cards," she said. "And I
certainly don't want to be a—"

"Of course, she'll have to go on a
diet," said Mr O'Brien, ignoring her.

"Dad—"

"And get her hair cut," said Mrs
O'Brien. "Perhaps we should dye it
blond."

"Mum—"

Mr O'Brien stood behind Katrina's
chair, then carefully pushed her ears
so that they pressed against her head.
"What d'you think? Do we need a
little operation to pin them back?"

"Maybe we should do something
about the nose at the same time."

"Mum, Dad, listen!" Shaking

herself free, Katrina stood up. "I don't
want to go on a diet, or have my hair
dyed blond, and I certainly don't
want a new nose. I'm happy the way
I am."

"Happy? What on earth has happy
got to do with it?" Mr O'Brien
frowned. "Don't you want to be a
very successful, very rich model?"

"No. It sounds dead boring."

Katrina's parents looked at one
another in amazement.

"I'll have you know that modelling
is a very skilled job, young lady," said
Mr O'Brien. "You have to walk up,
and then walk back. And, er, smile
quite a lot."

"Sounds the perfect job for you,"
said Mrs O'Brien. "Now the first
thing we have to do is pluck those
eyebrows of yours. Models always
have very small eyebrows. Yours look
like a couple of hedgehogs in a gale."

"What about the carpet, dear?" said Mr O'Brien. "It'll be littered with" – he shuddered – "plucked eyebrows."

"No gain without pain," said Mrs O'Brien, rummaging inside the household utilities bag that was never far from her, and taking out a pair of tweezers and a handkerchief. "I'll pluck and you catch," she said, giving the handkerchief to Mr O'Brien. "Then we'll go out and buy our little model some clothes for her audition."

Katrina decided to try once more. "What about my supper?"

"Good thinking, darling," said her mother. "We'll get some diet wafers while we're out."

Katrina groaned.

Shopping with her parents was never easy for Katrina, and that evening was no exception.

"The people," sniffed Mr O'Brien as they were jostled by shoppers carrying plastic bags.

"And the smell," said Mrs O'Brien. "Why can't everyone be nice and clean like us?"

They had been at the shopping centre for almost an hour. One clothes shop was too expensive. Another was too cheap. A third was much too vulgar. "Perhaps we should visit the High Street tomorrow, " Mrs O'Brien said finally. "They have some very acceptable shops there."

The three of them were just making their way down a small alleyway leading back to the car park when Katrina noticed a tumble-down clothes stall that she had never seen before. Brightly coloured shirts, skirts and dresses hung from it, making it look like an old-fashioned gypsy caravan. "Why don't we try here?" she asked.

Mr O'Brien laughed. "We are not buying your audition clothes from a market stall," he said firmly.

From behind the clothes, someone stirred. A woman wearing a wide-brimmed hat looked up. "Actually," she said, "it's not a market stall. It's an open-air boutique. We get all the top fashion labels – Armani, Gucci . . . er, Mitsubishi."

"I thought they made cars," said Katrina.

"Do they?" The woman looked a bit embarrassed. "Well, they're moving into clothes now. How about this one?" She held up a bright green dress.

Katrina smiled. Green was her favourite colour.

"Try it on, why don't you?" The woman with the hat nodded in the direction of a curtained-off cubicle behind the stall.

In the darkness, Katrina changed.

There was something about the woman's voice which brought back memories. Something about a rat at St Barnabas, was it? A school inspector? She looked at the dress, which fitted her perfectly. Stepping outside, she did a little twirl in front of her parents.

"Hm. Seems tidy enough," said her father.

"Isn't green a bit . . . vulgar?" asked her mother.

"It's not green, it's olive," said the stallholder, raising her voice slightly. "All the top designers are thinking olive this season. The word on Fashion Avenue is that olive is . . . way cool."

Katrina's parents looked at one another. "We'll take it," said Mrs O'Brien.

Katrina returned to the cubicle to change into her own clothes. Yes, she thought, there was definitely something odd about this little stall. The clothes had seemed almost too perfect – as if someone had read her mind and had known what sort of clothes she liked.

Then there was the stallholder. Katrina was certain that she had met her before. There was something about the way she talked – like an actor playing a part she had only just learnt – which seemed familiar.

"Shall I wrap it for you?" A hand reached in through the curtains. Katrina stared at it. On each of the fingernails was black nail-varnish.

"Ms Wiz?" she whispered.

"Ssh!" The hand grabbed the skirt and was gone.

Katrina stood in the darkness. Class Three's favourite paranormal operative had promised she would be there whenever magic was needed, but that didn't exactly explain what she was doing in a clothes stall at the local shopping centre.

Katrina smiled to herself. "Way cool, Ms Wiz," she said.

CHAPTER TWO

An Ordinary Old Mum

Podge Harris sat in the dining room at St Barnabas School. On the plate in front of him was piled a huge mountain of chips.

"Boy, do I like this modelling craze," he said to his friend Jack, who was sitting beside him. "Ever since all the girls decided to be skinny models, they've been giving me all their chips."

"Gross," said Jack.

Podge shrugged. "It's a tough job but someone's got to do it." As he was about to pick up his knife and fork, he noticed Katrina approaching their table. "Just pile the chips on top, Kat," he said casually.

"Forget it." Katrina sat down at the table, her head lowered. "I'm not starving myself for some French bloke with a silly name. I don't care what my parents say."

"Parents?" said Jack. "What have parents got to do with a fashion show?"

Katrina looked up angrily. "Some parents want their daughters to grow up to be models. Even when the daughters have always wanted to do something useful like being a doctor. Some parents see this fashion show as a way of making money out of their daughters."

Jack and Podge were staring at Katrina in amazement.

"What's the problem?" she asked. "Why shouldn't I be a doctor?"

"No problem," said Jack, nudging Podge. "Let's change the subject."

"No," said Katrina. " Why are you looking at me like that?"

One of the problems with Podge

Harris was that, when everyone else knew that the best, most sensible thing to do was to say nothing, he would speak his mind.

"It's your eyebrows." He peered more closely at Katrina. "They look like a couple of worms having a race down your nose."

Tears filled Katrina's eyes.

"Don't listen to Podge," said Jack. "I think your eyebrows look . . . really interesting."

"Yeah, that's what I meant," said Podge quickly. He speared half a dozen chips on to his fork.

"My mum did it," sniffed Katrina. "My parents have got this crazy idea that I'm going to be a child model and make their fortune. It's all they can talk about."

Podge and Jack thought for a moment.

"What you need is a bit of outside help," said Podge.

For the first time that day, Katrina smiled. "Funny you should mention that," she said. "Guess who I saw yesterday."

It had taken Jack and Podge all of ten seconds to reach their decision. Katrina had serious parent problems. Ms Wiz was working at a clothes stall. It was true that, the last time they had seen her, they had discovered that she was married to a school inspector and had a baby and had promised her husband not to cast any more spells, but then somehow Ms Wiz was always Ms Wiz even when she was calling herself Mrs Arnold.

It was time to pay her a visit.

Together, after school, Jack and Podge made their way through the shopping centre and down the small alley that Katrina had described. There, just where she had said it would be, was the clothes stall.

At first, as they approached, they thought there was no one looking after the stall. They looked at the brightly coloured clothes, the scarves, the wide-brimmed hat behind the counter.

"Jack! Podge!" A familiar voice came from under the hat. "Welcome to my little boutique."

"Ms Wiz?" Jack peered closer. "Are you under there?"

"How did she know it was us?" muttered Podge.

"Ms Wiz knows everything," said Ms Wiz, pushing the hat on to the back of her head.

"Thanks to magic, right?" said Jack.

"Wrong," said Ms Wiz. "Thanks to female intuition." She started rearranging some shirts on the table in front of her. "These days, I leave little baby William with Brian for a couple of days a week and earn a bit of extra money at this stall. I've always had a very strong fashion sense."

Jack and Podge looked at one another. They thought of the way Ms Wiz used to dress when she first taught at St Barnabas – the purple T-shirt, flashy jewellery, tight jeans. It may have been interesting – but it wasn't fashionable.

"I'd never thought of you as being exactly cool," said Jack carefully.

"You want cool?" said Ms Wiz sharply. "I'm beyond cool. I'm freezin'. I'm polar. I'm arctic, man!"

"We're a bit worried about Katrina," said Jack, changing the subject quickly. "Her parents are making her go to the auditions for this fashion extravaganza. They've put her on a diet and are talking about making her have an operation to pin her ears back and make her nose smaller."

"Mind you, it is a bit big," murmured Podge.

Ms Wiz smiled. "She'll look great at a fashion show. I sold her a lovely—"

"But she doesn't want to be a model," Podge explained.

"We were thinking that maybe you could come to the audition," said

Jack. "If anyone can help Katrina with her parents, you can."

"Help? But how? I've given up magic. You know I promised Brian I'd go straight."

"If you went to the audition," said Podge, "you could use your charm to persuade Mr and Mrs O'Brien that there's more to life than money."

"But I can't just turn up for the audition." Ms Wiz shook her head sadly. "I'm nothing more than an ordinary old mum these days."

"You're not ordinary," said Podge politely.

"And you're not old," said Jack. "In fact, you could probably get into the audition as a model yourself."

"Oh!" Ms Wiz fluttered her eyelashes and fluffed out her hair. "D'you really think so?"

"I'm going to try out for the fashion show too," said Jack. "I promised

Katrina I'd keep her company."

"Not an ordinary old mum at all," said Ms Wiz, looking at her reflection in a nearby mirror. "A model. A supermodel. I could be famous."

"And help Katrina," said Podge.

Ms Wiz turned towards a rack of clothes behind her. "I think I'll wear black," she said.

"And help Katrina," said Jack.

"I could wear my favourite yellow shoes," said Ms Wiz. "Yellow's *the* colour this year."

Podge and Jack looked at one another. "*And help Katrina!*" they said together.

Ms Wiz turned back to them slowly, as if something had suddenly occurred to her. "Maybe purple would be better," she said.

CHAPTER THREE

Wherps

"Silver play . . . silver play . . ."

A small man with short, greying
hair and extremely tight jeans was
standing in a corner of the St James
Church Hall. In front of him, paying
no particular attention, were about
fifty children and their parents.

"Silver *play*." He clapped his hands
in front of his face. Gradually the
buzz of conversation died down.
"Silver play is the French for 'please',
by the way."

"Stand up, we can't see you,"
called out one of the fathers in the
back row.

"I am standing up, Mr Fernny
Guy." The man clasped his hands in
front of him as if he was just about
to say a prayer. "Enough of ze rabbit-

rabbit-rabbit. It's tam to work. Or, as
we say in France, let's ger for eet."

In the front row, Katrina gave Jack
a cross-eyed, lemme-outta-here look.
Mr and Mrs O'Brien frowned at her.

"Moi ees . . . " the little man smiled,
revealing unnaturally white teeth,
"Yves de Chiqueville. You can call me
'maestro'. Today I am looking for
stars. But, maestro, you will say –
stars in ze daytime? Imposseeble! But
yes! Because ze stars I weell be seeing
are ze stars of ze catwalk!"

"What a weirdo," said Jack, rather
more loudly than he intended.

"So kiddies, here ees what I want
you to do. You walk zees way." Mr de
Chiqueville pranced across the floor.

"Walk that way? You must be
joking," muttered Jack.

"Zen you walk zat way." Mr de
Chiqueville skipped back like a ballet
dancer taking up his position. "You

walk, you smile, you act well natural,
OK? Ze winners will appear wiz
children from uzzer schools from ze
area in my Fashion Extravaganza at
ze Belmont Hotel next Saturday.
Tickets available at ze door."

Mrs O'Brien nudged her husband.

"Er, there was one thing, Mr de
Chiqueville," said Mr O'Brien.

"Monsieur?"

"The question of, er, remuneration.
We were wondering, well, how much
the successful kiddies would be
paid."

For a moment there was silence in
the church hall. Slowly, the fashion
designer walked up to Mr O'Brien.

"Leesten, meester," he said quietly.
"Moi ees one of ze world's greatest
designers. For zees show, I work
for nuzzing. Ze lighting, ze
choreographers, ze hotel, zey all geeve
zeir serveece for nuzzing. All ze

profits from tickets go to ze Chigwell Foundation, a well-known charity. Designers from all over ze world will come to my show – maybe zey choose your kiddie to be ze next supermerdel. But eef you want money from me, you can, how we say in France, sling your hook, mate. OK?"

"What's the charity for?" someone asked.

Mr de Chiqueville waved a hand. "Hospitals, homeless, donkeys – ze usual kind of thing. OK, let's ger. Parents, please stand back and let ze kiddies form a queue over zere."

Looking a bit self-conscious, the children stood in a line. Mr de Chiqueville reached under his chair and took out a radio cassette recorder. He switched it on and, as disco music started playing, the designer clapped his hands above his head. "Ger for eet!" he cried.

One by one, the children walked up
to the end of the room. Some just
wandered along, looking embarrassed.
Others tried vaguely to keep step
with the music.

When it was Jack's turn, he spun
around as if he were on his
skateboard, then did the cool-dude
walk which he used to do in the
playground. Katrina was laughing so
much that, when Jack returned to the
group and gave her the high five, she
skipped to the end of the room,
almost without thinking, did a twirl,
then ran back to the other children.

"Brilliant," said Mr O'Brien.

"Fabulous," said Mrs O'Brien.

Mr de Chiqueville switched off the
music and walked with brisk little
steps to where the children were
standing. He raised his right hand
like a magician and, walking down
the line, pointed at one child after

another. "Non . . . non . . . non . . . you merst be joking . . . non . . . non . . . oh, please, do me faveur . . . non . . ."

He only hesitated when he reached Jack. He looked at him thoughtfully. "Meester Show-off, huh?"

"Not really," said Jack.

"I lack."

"You lack what?"

"I lack zat vair much. Show me a show-off, I show you a merdel." He prodded Jack in the chest. "*Oui*," he said.

He turned to Katrina. "Lovely bone structure," he murmured. "And ze eyebrows are sheer heaven. *Oui* to you too."

"But—"

"Well done, darling," Mr O'Brien interrupted. "Now, Mr de Chiqueville, when do we—?"

There was a crash behind them and the double-doors flew open. There, in the doorway, stood a woman with long black hair combed so far forward that her face was almost invisible. She was wearing a sort of purple smock covered in patches and wide flared jeans. The high platform soles on her bright yellow shoes added about six inches to her height.

"Uh-oh." Jack nudged Katrina. "Guess who it is."

Everyone gazed in amazement as the figure shuffled forward, now and then tottering dangerously on her shoes. She looked down on Mr de Chiqueville and, extending a long finger with black nail-varnish, chucked him under the chin. "Mega," she said, brushing past him on her way to the radio cassette. "What's with the crusty sounds, grandad?"

Mr de Chiqueville squared his shoulders and tried to look taller than

he was. "I am nert your grandad," he said.

The woman had taken the tape out of the machine. She glanced at it, then threw it over her shoulder. She took a tape out of one of the many pockets in the smock. "Buzzin', kids." She twirled the tape in her fingers, then slotted it into the cassette. "This will knock your socks off."

Suddenly the room was filled with a sound like a hundred people falling down some stairs, screaming as they went.

"What ees zat?" shouted Mr de Chiqueville over the noise.

"Chill, guy." The woman was swaying slowly. "This is like a techno-hiphop-garage-heavy-housework club remix, right?" She walked the length of the room, moving like a sleepwalker, snapping her fingers. Because her hair was obscuring her eyes, she walked straight into the wall, bounced off, wheeled round, and tottered back.

"So?" She flicked off the music. "You dig?"

"Do I deeg? Are you crazy?" A stunned smile was on the designer's face. "You walk in here, I see you – you know the first thing I think? Boy, what a beeg berm."

Suddenly there was silence in the hall.

The woman walked slowly forwards. "What did you just say?"

"Uh-oh," murmured Jack again.

"I thought . . . I thought . . . " Mr de Chiqueville smiled nervously up at the woman. "I thought what a beeg bermb has exploded een here. You are a star!" He attempted to embrace the woman but she swatted him away like a fly. "Fifi, Zozo, Kate – eat your hearts out. Zis is ze real zing. What's your name, baby?"

"Baby?" The woman had stopped swaying. "Do I look like a baby?"

"Wherps," said Mr de Chiqueville.

"The name's Didi – Didi Wisteria."

"Didi. My faveureete name." The designer took Jack and Katrina by the arm. "Zese are ze uzzer two stars of my show."

"I'm Jack," said Jack.

"Mega."

"And I'm Katrina."

"Mega."

Jack and Katrina looked at one another. *Didi Wisteria*?

CHAPTER FOUR

Porkie-pie

It was breakfast time at the Belmont Hotel and, as they sat with Katrina and Jack, Mr and Mrs O'Brien were worried. They were worried that other people had once used the cups from which they were drinking. They were nervous about the fashion show which was due to happen that afternoon. And, as usual, they were very worried about money.

"Petrol . . . food . . ." Mr O'Brien tapped at the pocket calculator he always kept with him. "Plus £25 each for our tickets for the show. This is costing us a fortune."

"Mr de Chiqueville said it was an investment in Katrina's future as a model," groaned Mrs O'Brien. "I hope he's right."

Mr O'Brien looked at his watch. "Miss Wisteria is late already," he muttered. "I do hope she's not one of those untidy, disorganized people."

Katrina caught Jack's eye across the table. Ms Wiz may have had magic powers but tidiness and organization had never been her strong points.

At that moment, they became aware that several other of the guests were staring towards the door. Turning, they saw the unmistakable figure of Ms Wiz, otherwise known as Didi Wisteria. Today she was wearing a dazzling pink suit and dark glasses with bright green frames. She seemed to be talking into a small mobile telephone.

Peering through her hair, which hung like curtains over her face, she spotted the O'Briens and ambled across the dining room. She slumped on to the spare chair at their table, still talking into the telephone. "OK, babe, catch-ya-later, ciao." As she snapped the phone shut, it seemed to disappear into her hair.

"Make an entrance, why don't you," murmured Jack.

"Yo," said Ms Wiz to no one in particular.

"Good morning, Miss Wisteria," said Katrina's mother. "Did you have a good night?"

"Buzzin', babe," said Ms Wiz. "I was out clubbin' all night."

"That's nice," said Mr O'Brien.

"Haven't you been to bed at all?" asked Mrs O'Brien.

"Bed?" Ms Wiz lowered her dark glasses and smiled. "What's that?"

She sat down, then glanced around the room. "Why's everyone staring at me?" she muttered. "Anyone would think they had never seen a famous supermodel before."

A waiter, holding a small pad in front of him, approached the table. "Madam would like?" he said.

"No comment." Ms Wiz turned away from the waiter. "The press follow me everywhere these days," she said, shaking her head. "They just never ever leave me alone."

The waiter tried again. "What does madam want?" he asked.

"What do I want?" Ms Wiz sighed. "All right, get this down. First of all, I want world peace – like, an end to all this fighting in the world, right? And I feel really strongly about the rainforests. And whales, too. As for myself – well, right now I want to release a single, then maybe write a novel. And, no, I am not going to tell you if there's anyone special in my life."

The waiter frowned. "Would that be the full English breakfast, madam?"

Katrina leant across and whispered something in Ms Wiz's ear.

"A waiter?" For a moment, Ms Wiz seemed confused. "Of course I knew he was a waiter." She looked up. "Toast, please," she said coldly. "Very thinly sliced."

Mrs O'Brien leant across the table. "How long have you been a supermodel, Didi?" she asked.

Ms Wiz drew back some of the hair

covering her face, as if she was peering around a curtain. "How long is a piece of string?"

"We were wondering if you could advise us," said Mr O'Brien. "We're very keen that Katrina should pursue a career as a model and we were wondering . . . well, what kind of money she might expect."

"Money?"

"Just a ballpark figure," said Mrs O'Brien. "Would it be hundreds?" She gave a little shudder of pleasure. "Or thousands?"

Before Ms Wiz could reply, the bustling figure of Yves de Chiqueville could be seen making his way through the dining room towards them.

"Bonjour, bonjour," he trilled as he arrived at their table. "How are my leetle supermerdels?"

Jack and Katrina glanced at one

41

another. "Cool," said Ms Wiz.

Mr de Chiqueville laid a carefully manicured hand on Jack's shoulder. "But, before we start, I need Jack's signature for ze contract."

Jack frowned. "Contract?"

"Ees nuzzing to worry about, my leetle one. All my merdels have to sign a contract to say zey will reveal nuzzing about my shows. How zey work, ze cost of ze tickets. Ees normal. Trerst me."

Mrs O'Brien patted Katrina's hand. "Don't worry, love," she murmured. "We've signed for you."

Jack stood up. "I'll sign in a minute," he said. "I've just got to visit the bathroom." He smiled. "Stage fright, you know."

"Make it snappy, right?" Mr de Chiqueville called after Jack.

Ms Wiz cleared her throat loudly. "You'll be needing my signature, of course."

Mr de Chiqueville gave a wince of embarrassment. "Erm, non. Just ze younger generation. Ze contract ees for future shows."

Slowly Ms Wiz took off her dark glasses. "The younger generation?"

"Younger and, er, smaller. I lack my merdels nas and skinny. Modelling is for ze youth, non?"

"But you said Miss Wisteria was the real thing," protested Katrina.

The designer shrugged. "So I lad. I told ze leetle porkie-pie. Hey, ees business, non?"

"But she is in the show, right?" asked Katrina.

"Of cerse. Now and zen, I lack to include in my extravaganza a – how you say? – mature model. It helps to cheer up ze parents. Shows zat you're never too old to walk up and down in nas clothes." He glanced at his watch, and turned to go. "Be zere in twenty minutes, OK?"

"Mature." Ms Wiz spoke in a stunned voice as they watched Mr de Chiqueville skip out of the dining room. "He just called me mature."

"Makes you sound like a cheese," said Katrina, trying to break the tense atmosphere with a joke.

"Too old to walk the catwalk." Ms Wiz swept her hair back angrily.

"No magic, Ms Wiz," Katrina

murmured quietly. "Remember what you told Jack and Podge – you've gone straight."

Ms Wiz turned slowly and, for the first time, Katrina noticed that her normally green eyes had turned a dangerous bright blue. She smiled. "Did I really say that?"

CHAPTER FIVE

Arrest that Skeleton

In the Conference Centre of the
Belmont Hotel, a large audience had
gathered and was seated in rows on
three sides of a long catwalk which
led from a stage at the back of the
room. One larger chair, at the end of
the catwalk, had been left vacant. On
it, written in large letters, were the
words: *Reserved for Mr de Chiqueville.*
Occasionally, over the sound of the
audience's excited chatter, could be
heard the voice of an announcer,
speaking over the hotel intercom.

*"The show will commence in two
minutes."*

Mr and Mrs O'Brien sat in front-
row seats on one side of the catwalk.

"All these people!" said Mr
O'Brien. "I wonder how many are

top fashion designers looking out for new models."

"Most of them seem like parents to me," said Mrs O'Brien doubtfully.

Mr O'Brien nudged his wife. "Think of the money," he whispered.

"It's certainly making some money for Mr de Chiqueville's charity," muttered Mrs O'Brien. "He must have sold about 300 tickets."

"That's £7,500. But lots more than that for us when Katrina's a famous supermodel." Mr O'Brien rubbed his hands happily as the intercom announcer was heard once more.

"The show will commence in one minute."

"That Didi Wizzywazzy's a strange one," said Mrs O'Brien. "She became quite moody after Yves left us."

"Serves her right." Mr O 'Brien gave a superior little smile. "Calling herself a supermodel at her age."

"Her hair was *dreadfully* untidy."

"She should have settled down like us, shouldn't she? It's funny how some people just can't seem to grow up."

"What was all that stuff about magic?"

"Magic?" Mr O'Brien crossed his arms and looked around him as if daring anyone to disagree with him. "The only magic that's worth anything in this life is the magic of a tidy house and a healthy bank balance."

Nearby, there was a stir of interest as Mr de Chiqueville took his seat.

"*Ladies and gentlemen, the Yves de Chiqueville Fashion Extravaganza is about to commence.*"

The lights grew dim. The music swelled. The audience was quiet. Spotlights lit up the catwalk.

Five children wearing sports clothes ran on and danced in time to the music.

"Brackenhurst School are modelling new designs from Gary, the big name in sportswear," said the announcer. As the children ran off, there was applause from the audience.

The music changed and three older girls walked on, wearing shellsuits and tanktops.

"Jesse, Kate and Raksha from Broadhurst Comprehensive, wearing the hottest fashions from the Jazz Boutique. Check it out!"

More applause. As the music changed again, Jack and Katrina ran on in jeans and T-shirts.

"Modelling the best in leisurewear from Blazes Boutique, Jack and Katrina from St Barnabas."

"Brilliant," cried Mr O'Brien above the sound of the clapping.

"Bravo!" called out Mrs O'Brien.

"And for parents who are still young at heart . . ."

The music seemed to be fading to be replaced by a loud, and rather strange, humming sound.

". . . *Didi Wisteria!*"

Slowly Ms Wiz walked on to the stage – a stunning, dramatic sight in purple and black, her eyes glowing blue in the spotlight.

"*Didi is wearing—*"

But suddenly, instead of the announcer, the voice of Yves de Chiqueville came over the intercom.

"*I like my merdels nas and skinny.*"

Ms Wiz smiled at Mr de Chiqueville. "You want skinny?" she said.

Behind her, there appeared three figures in elegant black silk cloaks with hoods hiding their faces. Ms Wiz raised a hand. For a brief second, there was silence in the room. When she let the hand fall, the figures pulled their hoods back to reveal – three skulls.

There was a gasp from some members of the audience. "Excellent make-up," said Mr O'Brien nervously.

As the figures moved towards the catwalk, they let their gowns fall to the floor. It was now three skeletons who walked forward slowly, their bones glinting in the spotlight.

"V-v-very clever," said Mr O'Brien. "It's almost as if they are—" He turned to his wife, just in time to see her eyes fluttering as she slipped from her chair in a dead faint.

The first scream came from the back of the room. Within seconds, there was a stampede towards the door. Mr de Chiqueville stood on a chair. "Dern't paneec," he shouted above the uproar. "Ees a wind-up. Ees just a—" He noticed that one of the skeletons was moving closer. "Bloomin' 'eck, I'm outta here."

He jumped down from the chair, scurried towards a side door and pulled it open – to find himself staring into the large uniformed chest of a police officer.

Slowly, the policeman rested his hand on the designer's shoulder. "Hullo, Izzy," he said, almost kindly. "Going somewhere?"

"Sank goodness you're here, officer." Mr de Chiqueville pointed over his shoulder. "Arrest zose skeletons."

Casually, the policeman looked towards the catwalk. Ms Wiz stood alone. She smiled, waved, then turned to leave the stage.

"Arrest a skeleton? There's only one person being arrested around here," said the policeman. "And it ain't no skeleton."

"There's been a terrible mistake." Mr O'Brien appeared, his wife resting palely on his arm. "This is Yves de

54

Chiqueville, the famous designer."

The policeman laughed. "Otherwise known as Izzy from Chigwell, the famous conman who's about as French as I am. It's his favourite trick – travelling around the country, setting up fashion shows."

"He said it was for charity."

"In a way it is for charity," said the policeman. "It's the Get-Izzy-A-Really-Nice-Holiday-In-Majorca Appeal. He's clever at getting money out of stupid parents who

want their kids to be models."

"Stupid?" Mrs O'Brien seemed to be recovering from her faint. "What's stupid about that?"

"Sometimes I think it's them I should be arresting," said the policeman. "A night in a dirty cell would do them no end of good."

"Cell?" said Mrs O'Brien.

"Dirty?" said Mr O'Brien.

"Only kidding." The policeman winked. "I think they've learnt their lesson."

Mrs O'Brien nodded. "Yes, I think we – I mean, they – have."

Jack and Katrina appeared from backstage. "No more modelling, darling," said Mr O'Brien. He smiled nervously at the policeman. "Kids! Sometimes they're too ambitious for their own good, aren't they?"

"Who grassed on me?" muttered Izzy angrily.

"We had a tip-off earlier today," said the policeman. "A young man rang the station from the hotel. Said there was something strange going on. We checked on the police computer and there was Izzy."

"Bloomin' copper," said Izzy.

The policeman pushed him towards the door. "These Frenchmen." He shook his head. "No manners at all."

"Nice one, Jack," said Katrina as they collected their clothes in the backstage area. "How did you know about Izzy?"

"He was well dodgy, that bloke," said Jack. "Twenty-five quid a ticket? Then when he wanted us to sign a contract promising to keep quiet, I thought it was worth a call to the boys in blue."

"It certainly scared my mum and dad."

Ms Wiz swept in, still in purple and black. "I think you'll find it was my skeletons that did the trick," she said.

"So much for there being no magic," laughed Katrina.

Ms Wiz smiled. "I just couldn't help myself," she said. "Promise not to tell Brian."

"Your secret's safe with us," said Katrina.

"Talking of secrets," said Jack. "All that stuff about you being mature made me think. How old *are* you exactly?"

"I'd better get changed back into my normal clothes," said Ms Wiz, stepping quickly into a small dressing room.

"We wouldn't tell," Jack called out through the half-closed door.

"It can't be that bad," said Katrina. "You're a paranormal operative. You should be above worrying about how old you are."

There was silence from next door.

"Ms Wiz?" said Katrina.

No reply.

Slowly Jack opened the door to the adjoining room where Ms Wiz had gone. There was no one there.

"Look," said Katrina. "She's written a load of numbers in pink lipstick across the mirror. It must be her telephone number."

"I somehow don't think so," said Jack.

"Actually . . ." As if coming to them from a great distance, the voice of Ms Wiz could be heard from behind the mirror. "It's the age I'll be on my next birthday."

"Oh yeah, right," said Katrina. "So you were a paranormal operative in the days of cavemen, I suppose."

"Charming people." The voice was growing fainter now. "If a little rough."

There was silence. For a few seconds, Jack and Katrina stood staring at the mirror, from which the numbers written in lipstick were already fading.

"See you, Didi," said Katrina.

"You've got to hand it to Ms Wiz." Jack smiled. "She doesn't look at all bad for her age."

MS WIZ GOES
TO HOLLYWOOD

CHAPTER ONE

The Queen of Sheba

Shelley Kelly was sitting between her mother and her older sister Kate. It was the first day of half-term and she was in a bad mood. All that morning she had been looking forward to watching an old film called *A Star is Born* which was on TV that afternoon but, as soon as lunch had finished, Kate and her mum had switched on a stupid daytime show called *Just How Weird Is That?* Right now, on the screen, a man and a woman were shouting at one another while people in the audience screamed and laughed.

"This is the saddest thing I've ever seen," Shelley muttered.

"If you don't like it, you can go to

your room, Shelley Kelly," said her mother briskly.

"But it's *A Star is Born*," Shelley protested. "I had been looking forward to that film all day."

"Two against one," said Kate smugly. "It's called democracy."

"It's called unfair." Shelley's eyes filled with tears. As far as she could see, all that democracy meant was that, in her own family, she never ever got what she wanted. Sometimes she would sit in her room, going through her celebrity scrapbook, and try to imagine what her life would be like if she had been born into a home like the ones she saw in films. Her mother would laugh at her jokes and they would make home-made chocolate cookies together in a big kitchen and have giggly conversations at bedtime and she would never ever have to worry about having a bossy older sister because she would be a much-loved only child. And every afternoon after school, a few of her funny, good-looking friends would come round to play with her in the garden as the sun shone and the birds sang in the trees and—

"Phone." A sharp dig in the ribs from Kate awoke Shelley from her daydream. From outside in the corridor, she heard the ringing of the telephone.

"Be a love, Shell," said her mother, lighting up a cigarette.

Shelley stood up, wandered out of the room and picked up the receiver.

"Could I speak to Miss Shelley Kelly?" It was the voice of a man. He sounded strangely excited.

"This is Shelley Kelly speaking."

"Am I right in thinking that you

entered the *Celeb! Magazine* Fan of the Year contest?"

Shelley frowned. She was always entering quizzes and competitions but she was really not sure if she could remember that one. "Maybe," she said uncertainly.

"Yowee! I'm delighted to tell you that you are the winner of our all-star competition. Start packing your bags right now – you're on your way to

Hollywood for a week, all expenses paid!"

Shelley pulled sharply at her nose in order to wake herself up.

"This is not a dream," said the man, as if he could read her mind.

"But I'm only ten years old," Shelley said.

"No problem. In a few minutes' time, my colleague Diamante Wisporina will arrive at your door. She will be your special guide to Hollywood."

"But—"

"Cheerio, Shelley, old bean. Have a great time in Tinsel City." And the man was gone.

Shelley walked slowly back to the sitting room.

"Who was that?" asked her mother, without taking her eyes away from the screen.

"It was a man telling me I had won

a competition to go to Hollywood."

"Get a life," muttered Kate.

"Honestly, Shell," sighed Mrs Kelly. "You and your daydreams."

Just then, the doorbell rang. Grumbling, Mrs Kelly stubbed out her cigarette and went to answer it.

A woman wearing a baseball cap and bright purple dark glasses stood on the doorstep. "My name is Diamante Wisporina," she said. "And I'm here to take a Miss Shelley Kelly to Hollywood."

"Diamante who?" Mrs Kelly asked a few moments later as the Kelly family sat together on the sofa in the sitting room.

"Wisporina," said the woman. As she took off her glasses, Shelley noticed that she had black nail varnish on her fingernails. "But my friends call me Ms Wiz."

Ms Wiz? Ever since Shelley had arrived at St Barnabas School a few months before, she had heard stories about the mysterious woman with special powers who used to appear whenever magic was needed. No one had seen her for a long time and the rumour at school had been that the famous Ms Wiz had given up spells to be a wife and mother.

"I used to be a teacher," Ms Wiz continued. "Then I, er, did one or two other things. Now I work for *Celeb! Magazine.*"

"Well you can be the Queen of Sheba as far as I'm concerned," said Mrs Kelly firmly. "No way am I going to allow my little daughter to spend half-term on the other side of the world with a total stranger."

Ms Wiz laughed. "But I'm not a stranger. They know me at St Barnabas. When I saw that someone from Class Five had won the big prize, I decided to take her to Hollywood myself."

"Aren't you supposed to be a magician or something?" Shelley asked uncertainly.

"A paranormal operative actually," said Ms Wiz. "But I've retired from magic." She reached into the bag which was slung over her shoulder and took out two telephones – one purple and one yellow. "And this is a gift from the magazine to the other members of Shelley's family."

Suspiciously, Mrs Kelly and Kate put the phones to their ears. At that moment, a faint humming noise could be heard coming from them. Slowly they turned back to the television and

sat motionless, a distant smile on their faces. On the screen, the people on *Just How Weird Is That?* were frozen into immobility.

"Er, Ms Wiz," said Shelley Kelly. "About that business of retiring from magic—"

Ms Wiz glanced at her watch. "We have just stepped out of normal time," she said briskly. "I've got you a bag of clothes, a passport and tickets and our flight is about to leave."

"Flight?" Shelley shook her head in disbelief. "But I can't leave my mother and sister sitting like a couple of zombies."

Ms Wiz smiled. "When you return, they won't even know that you've been gone. You will literally be back in no time."

A humming noise vibrated in the air. Shelley Kelly hesitated. It worried her that, all the time she was away, her mother and Kate would be sitting there staring blankly at *Just How Weird Is That?* On the other hand, she thought, they would probably be doing that anyway.

The humming noise sounded louder.

"The glitter, the glamour, the chance to meet famous celebrities and discover what Hollywood is really like," whispered Ms Wiz. "What can possibly go wrong? All you have to do is touch my hand."

Shelley reached out. "Bye, Mum and Kate," she said quietly. "I'll see you in a minute."

Her fingers touched those of Ms Wiz. There was the sound of rushing wind in her ears, a sensation of flying at great speed. Then everything went black.

CHAPTER TWO

Like, A Magic Thing?

Shelley Kelly opened her eyes. She
was seated in a big leather chair,
which was in a sort of cabin with a
low roof, rows of seats and small
circular windows. She turned to Ms
Wiz, who sat beside her, eyes closed
and still holding on to her hand.

"Er, Ms Wiz," she said. "We seem to
be in a plane."

"Correct," Ms Wiz spoke quietly.
"We are in the first class seats of Flight
7468 to Los Angeles." She squeezed
Shelley's hand more tightly. "Just tell
me when we've taken off."

Shelley frowned. "You can't be
nervous. I heard that you were
always flying around on vacuum

76

cleaners or chairs."

"That's proper flying," said Ms Wiz. "This is just plain unnatural."

At that moment, the curtains at the front of the plane drew back. A man and a woman, both wearing dark glasses and with white scarves concealing half their faces, were shown to the two seats across the aisle.

As they settled down, carefully taking off their scarves, Shelley looked more closely at them. There was something about the man that seemed vaguely familiar – the suntan, the long floppy hair, the thin sideburns which curled to a neat point on his perfect high cheekbones.

He had taken off his dark glasses and was adjusting his hair when he noticed that he was being watched. "Uh-oh," he said in a voice just loud enough for Shelley to hear. "Fan alert."

"Relax," said the woman, checking her make-up in a pocket mirror. "She'll be looking at me, not you," she said.

"Oh please, she is so not looking at you." The man gave a snickering little laugh. "That's a Bradette, if ever I saw one."

Shelley gasped as she remembered where she had last seen the couple – she had been sticking a photograph of them into her celebrity scrapbook.

"Ms Wiz," she hissed. "Across the aisle. It's Brad Le Touquet and Lori Angelo."

"Mm?" Outside the jets roared and the plane began to move forward.

"They're the most famous, glamorous, romantic film star couple in the world."

Ms Wiz held Shelley's hand so tightly that it hurt. She seemed to be praying.

*

Shelley was finding it difficult to concentrate. A few moments ago, she had been sitting at home, feeling bored. Now she was on a jet flying to America, with Ms Wiz on one side and, on the other, two of her favourite movie stars.

There were so many things that she wanted to ask Brad and Lori. Was it true that they had been childhood sweethearts? Had Lori cried real tears when Brad's character was hurt in a car crash in *Miracles Can Happen*? Did Brad feel jealous when Lori had to kiss another actor in a film? What was their favourite food? Could she have their autographs?

Unfortunately, the famous film star couple did not seem to be in the mood for conversation. Soon after take-off, Lori had complained about the type of champagne being served. Then Brad discovered that none of their films were being shown during the flight. Now they were just lying back in their seats, with white eye-shields over their eyes, saying nothing.

Suddenly, Brad sat up. "Something ran over my foot," he said.

"Yeah, right," Lori murmured from behind her eye-shield. "I warned you about those pills you're taking."

"It so did! It was like some kind of—" Brad shuddered, "creature."

Lori raised her eye-shield. "Hey, why don't you do what you do in restaurants and just walk out?" she said. "The exit is over there."

Shelley turned to Ms Wiz. She was just about to tell her that Brad and Lori seemed rather different in real life from their public image when she noticed that, sitting on the armrest beside her, was a rat. It seemed to be wearing dark glasses.

"Pleased to meet you, old bean," he said to Shelley. "The name's Herbert." He nodded in the direction of Ms Wiz. "I'm partner to Lady Muck here. I say 'partner' – between you and me, I run the show while she takes all the credit."

"Thank you, Herbert," murmured Ms Wiz.

"Oh yes," Herbert continued. "It was me who rang you up, of course."

Shelley blinked. "You rang me?"

"Yowee! I'm delighted to tell you that you are the winner of our all-star competition."

To Shelley's astonishment, the voice was exactly that of the man who had called her at home.

"I'm very, very good at voices." Herbert lay back and started to sing. "California, here I come. Lots of

champagne in my tum."

Ms Wiz opened her eyes and looked at him sharply. "Champagne? So that's where you've been, Herbert. I wondered where you had sneaked off to."

The rat yawned and stretched out on the armrest. "Free champers for first-class passengers. Not a bad tipple, as it happens."

"Oh, my goodness." It was the voice of Brad le Touquet. "Where did you get that cute toy?"

Herbert turned slowly. "Toy, sir? I'll have you know that I'm as real as you are." He lowered his sunglasses and seemed to be staring at Brad's hair. "Possibly more real, if you know what I mean."

Lori Angelo laughed. "That's a great act," she said to Ms Wiz. "How d'you work him?"

Ms Wiz shrugged. "It's a long story," she said. "I was born with these special paranormal powers which allow me to do things that other people find unusual – fly, change shape, move through time, keep a talking rat."

"Like, a magic thing?" asked Brad, who was still nervously running his hands through his hair.

"You call it magic, I call it life."

"You're in the business, right?" said Brad. "Who's your agent?"

"Agent?" Ms Wiz laughed modestly. "Shelley and I are just ordinary people on our way to take a look around Hollywood." She paused, then added casually, "I probably won't even mention the book I'm writing – *There's No Business Like Ms Wizness – My Life as a Paranormal Operative* by Dolores Wisdom."

"Magic's very big in Hollywood right now," Brad said thoughtfully. "Is there a really great, handsome, hunky male hero in your book?"

"Well, there's my husband, Mr Arnold. He's a school inspector," said Ms Wiz.

"Does he ride a motorbike, drink beer from the bottle, get in fights now and then, forget to shave in the

morning? Is he kinda wild and kinda lost, yet deep down a really sensitive guy who's just looking for true love?"

Ms Wiz thought for a moment. "Not exact—"

"Yes, that's him," interrupted Shelley, nudging Ms Wiz. "That sums him up perfectly."

Lori Angelo was smiling. "I can see it now. A great new movie for all the family. *There's No Business Like Ms Wizness*, starring Lori Angelo as Ms Wiz. With Brad Le Touquet as Mr Arnold."

"I prefer *Mr Arnold* as a title," said Brad. "I can see the posters now. Brad Le Touquet *is* Mr Arnold." He leant across Shelley as if she didn't exist. "Dolores." He gazed sincerely into Ms Wiz's eyes. "I feel there is something very special going on here," he said. "Will you promise not to mention this idea to anyone before we talk in Hollywood?"

"Of course," said Ms Wiz.

Lori Angelo sat back in her seat. "I've always wanted to play a witch," she murmured.

"Tell me about it," said Brad.

CHAPTER THREE

So One of the Team

Shelley Kelly was in paradise. During her first day she had visited two studios, eaten the biggest hamburger she had ever seen and had spotted Leonardo DiCaprio (or someone who looked very much like him) driving by in an open-topped limousine. When they returned to the Belair Hotel, where they were staying, there were three messages at the hotel desk.

The first read: *Courtney, Brad Le Touquet's personal assistant, rang about the Wiz project. Please ring 333.4561.* The second read: *Mel, Brad Le Touquet's producer, rang re Wiz project. Call him any time, day or night.* The third read simply: *Brad rang. Let's talk soonest.*

Ms Wiz smiled as she casually stuffed the messages into her back pocket. "When you're hot, you're hot," she said.

"Who will you ring first?" asked Shelley. "Courtney, Mel or Brad?"

"None of them." Ms Wiz walked briskly towards the lift. "Remember the first rule of show business. Treat 'em mean, keep 'em keen."

As they entered their room on the 33rd floor, the telephone was ringing. Ms Wiz waited for a while before picking up the receiver. "Ms Wiz speaking," she said casually. "Ah hello, Brad . . . Yes, I got the messages – we've just come back from the Twentieth Century Fox studios."

From where Shelley stood, she could hear Brad Le Touquet's agitated voice.

"No, no." Ms Wiz laughed. "We

weren't talking to them about my book. We were just looking around." She nodded. "Meeting tomorrow. Your car will pick us up at ten? That's fine. Oh—" Suddenly, she seemed to be blushing. "And you're very sweet, too." Slowly, she put the phone down.

"Er, Ms Wiz?" Shelley frowned. "Did I hear you tell Brad Le Touquet that he was sweet?"

"I was just being polite," said Ms Wiz in a distant voice. "That's the way we talk in showbusiness. He told me I was a very special person."

"You don't think that maybe he's just a tiny bit false?" Shelley asked carefully.

"False?" Ms Wiz spoke in a dreamy, distant voice. "What on earth is false about him?"

"Darling, honey, Dolores, light of my

life – I haven't been able to *sleep* for thinking of you."

Brad Le Touquet bounded across the office where they met the next morning and held Ms Wiz in his arms for several seconds.

"Hello, Brad." Ms Wiz extricated herself from the film star's arms. "You remember Shelley?"

"Hi, kid." Brad nodded briefly in Shelley's direction, then turned to a long table where a man and a woman, each perfectly tanned, were sitting. "This is Mel and Courtney – my people."

"Our people," muttered Lori Angelo, who was sitting in a corner reading a magazine.

"Whatever," said Brad, flouncing around the table and taking a seat between Mel and Courtney.

"Dolores." Mel gazed across the

table and seemed for a moment as if he were about to cry. "Brad and Lori have told us all about you and—" he glanced at Shelley, "your little friend. I have to say we all feel privileged and moved to have heard your amazing story. It's funny, exciting, warm and, with Lori and Brad on board, it's gonna make audiences go home with hope in their hearts and a song in their soul." He paused, as if the emotion was all too much for him, then pulled himself together. "What was it about again?"

Ms Wiz sat forward, then began talking. "My book *There's No Business Like Ms Wizness* is going to tell the story of my life – how I was born a few thousand years ago into a family of paranormal operatives, and going right through to today when I spend most of my time with my lovely husband Mr Arnold and my little boy William, now and then visiting my friends at St Barnabas School."

"Like, *Buffy the Vampire-Slayer* meets *Honey, I Shrunk the Kids*," said Courtney. "I like it already."

"This is so my kind of project," murmured Brad.

"Of course, although I do have strange and amazing special powers, I only use magic when it is needed," Ms Wiz continued. "For example, when my friend Podge was turned into a zombie slave and taken into the underworld by my evil sister Barbara. Or when my talking rat Herbert fell in love and needed rescuing from the local Environmental Health Officer. Or when Jack travelled back in time and got lost in history. You know, little everyday things."

"*The X-files* meets *Dr Dolittle* and

The Time Bandits," said Courtney.

"That's great, Dolores." Mel smiled and the room seemed to be illuminated by his dazzling white teeth. "But, you know, we're in the moving picture business. We need to be able to see these characters. Who is this Podge, this Herbert, this Jack? How will they play in a film?"

"How would they play?" Ms Wiz closed her eyes, and a faint humming sound filled the room. Within seconds, the table seemed to be covered in a sort of mist. When it cleared, three glasses of sparkling water that were on the table appeared to be full of moving characters.

"This is Podge," said Ms Wiz, pointing to the first glass where a rather large boy could be seen cramming a slice of pizza into his mouth as he watched TV. She moved

to the second glass where a father
could be seen reading a picture book
to a baby. "That's my own Mr Arnold
and William," she said. "And this—"
She looked at the third glass in which
Herbert could be seen lapping
something from a saucer. "Oh dear,
that's Herbert back at the hotel and he
seems to have got hold of some
champagne from the minibar."

Slowly the pictures faded.

"Sheesh." Mel picked up the glass in front of him. "No way am I going to drink that water. It's had people in it."

In the corner, Lori had looked up from her magazine. "Lose the rat," she said coolly.

"But you can't make a film about Ms Wiz without the famous Herbert," Shelley protested.

Mel winced. "Here's the thing," he said. "Rodents are bad box-office right

now. And a rat with a drink problem –
well, that's gonna be a toughie
whichever way you look at it."

"Maybe I could turn him into something else," said Ms Wiz. "A dog,
perhaps."

"That's it. Brilliant!" Mel clicked his
fingers. "A cuddly, cute little mutt
that's always doing the darnedest
things."

"*Benji* meets *The Witches*," said
Courtney.

Mel pushed a sheet across the table
towards Ms Wiz. "Get your people to
look over our contract and get right
back to us," he said.

"People?" said Ms Wiz. "We *are* our
people. I'm sure your contract is
absolutely lovely."

There was a brief, astonished
silence.

"Lovely? Our contract?" Mel

laughed rather too loudly. "Yeah, right. It's one of the wonders of the world."

Brad Le Touquet held out a pen to Ms Wiz. "You are so one of the team now, Dolores," he said.

"Ms Wiz," said Shelley urgently. "Wouldn't it be a good idea to read what it says first?"

Brad half-turned towards her and narrowed his eyes. "When we need the advice of some little Bradette, I'm sure you'll be the first to know."

"What's a Bradette, Brad?" asked Ms Wiz as she signed the contract.

CHAPTER FOUR

Spells-'n'-Smoochin'

Shelley Kelly was worried. It was two days since Ms Wiz had signed the contract, and since then she had been behaving more and more oddly. Most of the time she spent telling the story of her life into a small tape machine. Whenever the telephone rang, she started and said "It's Brad!" and ran to pick it up. But the call was always from Mel who was asking whether he could pick up the tape she had been making.

On the morning of her third day in Hollywood, Shelley stood at the window of the Belair. Behind her, she heard the voice of Ms Wiz, as she dictated her story. "I'll never forget the day when I first turned a headteacher into a warthog," she was saying. "My, how we laughed when . . ."

On the other side of the room, Herbert was preparing for his big break in films as a dog. "Woof," he said. "Sniff, sniff, sniff, woof. Oh look, there's a nice telegraph pole. I think I'll lift my leg—"

"You don't have to go that far, Herbert," Shelley shouted.

"Rover, if you don't mind," said Herbert. "In order to be a dog, I have to feel like a dog, think like a dog, even smell like a dog."

"You've managed that already," muttered Ms Wiz.

"It's called method acting," said Herbert, ignoring her. "I'll probably win an Oscar for best supporting rat. I can see the headlines: HERBERT RAISES THE WOOF."

There was a knock on the hotel door.

"It's Brad!" Ms Wiz squealed, jumping up from the bed and checking her hair in the mirror. But when Shelley opened the door, it was Mel who was standing there, with Courtney just behind him.

"Yo, people." Mel wandered into the room. Courtney was about to follow when she gave a little scream.

With a shaking hand, she pointed to the dressing-table where Herbert was sitting up and begging with a matchstick in his mouth.

"Don't worry," said Shelley. "It's only Herbert pretending to be a dog."

Courtney looked more closely. "Like *Supermouse* meets *101 Dalmatians*? That is just so wacky."

Ignoring Ms Wiz, Mel picked up the tape recorder that had been lying on the bed and passed it to Courtney. "We need this right now," he said. "Our writers are standing by to get started."

"But I'm still in the early years," Ms Wiz protested. "My very first spell. Memories of my lovely sisters. The day I met the children of Class Three at St Barnabas."

"Yeah, yeah." The producer glanced at his watch. "Maybe we'll give you another tape machine for the other stuff. Meantime, I've got a movie to produce."

Shelley stared at Mel. He had definitely changed since Ms Wiz had signed the contract. Before he had been all smiles but now he seemed brisk and impatient. "Why is there so much hurry?" she asked.

Mel looked down at Shelley, hands on hips. "What is it with you, kid? How come you always make with the negative questions? Just trust us, right?"

"But it is Ms Wiz's story," said Shelley.

"Correction." Mel smiled nastily. "Was Ms Wiz's story. She signed the contract. It's ours now."

Ms Wiz frowned. "I think I'd better talk to Brad about this."

"He's not taking calls," said Mel.

Courtney stepped forward. "The

truth is, we've got a situation," she said, opening her briefcase and taking out a newspaper. "This is yesterday's *Hollywood Reporter*."

Shelley took the newspaper. On its front page, beneath a picture of Brad and Lori, a headline read: "WITCH HITCH TAKES FIZZ OUT OF WIZ BIZ."

"What on earth does that mean?" Shelley asked.

"Don't they teach kids English where you come from?" Mel grabbed the paper and began to read. "Within days of the announcement that Hollywood's finest, Brad Le Touquet and Lori Angelo, have committed to *Wizzed*, a major new spells-'n'-smoochin' feature, the project is in trouble. The story of zany screwball Ms Wiz, to be played by Lori, and her on–off relationship with Brad's character, a washed-up stuntman called Mr Arnold, is said by its critics to be a witch too far. 'These stars are role models for our children,' commented Ted Strait, whose Society for Disturbed, Angry Parents, or SDAP!, has vowed to clean up Hollywood. 'We've heard that, in this film, they'll be changing people into warthogs, flying though time and even descending to the underworld. What kind of example is that to our kids? SDAP! says stop this weird stuff before it gets out of hand.' "

"How ridiculous," said Shelley. "What harm can a bit of magic do?"

"Truth is, we've gotta head this thing off at the pass," said Mel. "So here's the deal. We've booked you on to tomorrow's *Just How Weird Is That?* show. We want you both to go on nationwide TV and make like you're completely harmless."

"Woof, me, woof, on the show?" asked Herbert.

"You're kidding," said Mel. "We got enough problems without fielding an alcoholic talking rat who thinks he's a dog."

"I'm going to be on *Just How Weird Is That?*" Shelley laughed. "Mum won't believe it."

"The only way we got you on the

show was to agree that Brad and Lori will be there too," said Mel. "Then there will be the guy from SDAP!" He walked to the door, followed by Courtney. "It'll be fine – just let Brad and Lori do the charm thing while you act normal."

It was not until they had gone that Shelley noticed that Ms Wiz had turned very pale.

"Harmless, Ms Wiz. Act normal." Shelley smiled encouragingly. "We can manage that, can't we?"

"*Wizzed*?" Ms Wiz stared into space. "On–off relationship with a stuntman? A zany screwball? Just wait until Brad hears about this!"

"What is it that tells me he knows already?" said Shelley.

From across the room, Herbert growled.

CHAPTER FIVE

Ditch the Witch

Shelley Kelly was sitting with Ms Wiz in a small room behind the *Just How Weird Is That?* studios, watching the start of the programme on a TV monitor. In a few minutes' time, they had been told, they would be taken into the studio. In the meantime, Brad, Lori and Ted Strait from the Society for Disturbed, Angry Parents were on stage and were being introduced by the show's host Jermaine Chance.

"Tonight we have with us the world's favourite, most romantic film star couple." Jermaine gave a big TV smile in the direction of Brad and Lori who were sitting, holding hands, on the stage. "And we also have Mr Ted

Strait who says they've got to SDAP!
what they're doing for the sake of our
kids." The camera panned to a
smiling, middle-aged man in a dark
suit.

"Because, guess what? Brad and
Lori have gone all witchy on us,"
Jermaine continued. "They'll be
making spells and all kinds of spooky
stuff for *Wizzed*, their next major
movie. Later we'll be meeting the
person who gave them the idea, a lady
who claims to be a real witch and we'll
be asking—" She held up her hands
like the conductor of an orchestra at
the start of a symphony.

"JUST HOW WEIRD IS THAT?"
shouted the audience.

"I don't like the sound of this," said
Shelley to Ms Wiz.

But Ms Wiz was not listening. "You
know, they're only holding hands

because they're in front of the cameras," she said, staring at the screen. "That whole Brad and Lori thing is history," she said.

"Ms Wiz," Shelley spoke gently. "I think that right now you should remember that you are a happily married woman with a lovely young baby. Falling in love with a film star is a really bad idea."

"Love?" Ms Wiz laughed girlishly. "It's much too early to talk about love. It's just one of those holiday romances. I can't help it if Brad has . . . special feelings towards me."

Shelley was about to point out that, as far she could see, the only special feelings that Brad seemed to have were for himself when the assistant director appeared at the door. "You're on," she said.

*

Moments later, Shelley and Ms Wiz were waiting behind a curtain at the back of the stage as Jermaine Chance spoke to the audience.

"OK, so our next guest claims to be thousands of years old," she said to laughter from the audience. "She says she has magic powers." Someone shouted, "Oh, yeah, right" to more laughter. "And now she's here to tell us that what she does is all a bit of fun. Please welcome, here with her young friend Shelley Kelly . . . Ms Wiz!"

The curtain drew back. As Ms Wiz and Shelley stepped into the lights to take their seats on stage, the sound of booing and laughter was deafening. At the back of the studio, someone held up a placard with the words "DITCH THE WITCH!" written on it.

"So, Ms Wiz." Jermaine stood at the front of the stage, a serious expression

on her face. "Let me get this straight.
You're a witch, right?"

"Wrong." Ms Wiz's eyes flashed
dangerously. "Witches are old-
fashioned and boring. I am a modern
paranormal operative – an everyday
person who just happens to have a few
unusual powers. Otherwise—" she
darted a shy smile at Brad, "I'm just an
ordinary woman."

"Witch, wizard, paranormal opera-

tive – it's all the same." Ted Strait
spoke directly to the audience. "It
sounds like a bit of innocent fun but
what disturbed, angry parents want to
know is what all this hocus-pocus is
doing to our kids. OK, so first they
play around with a bit of so-called
magic. Then they start dabbling with
potions. Before you know it, they'll be
caught up in a world of voodoo, weird
spells and ritual sacrifices of the family

pet at the end of the garden."

As the audience applauded, a man at the back of the studio stood up and Jermaine Chance held up her microphone to him. "I'm one of Brad and Lori's greatest fans," he said. "I want to ask them why they have allowed themselves to get involved with all this crazy magic stuff."

Lori smiled. "I can promise our millions of fans that the main magic in this film is going to be the romance between Brad's character Mr Arnold and me. Isn't it, Brad?"

"Sure thing, honey – the spells are just a joke." When Brad spoke, Shelley noticed that his voice seemed to be deeper than it had been in real life. "Basically *Wizzed* is about the relationship between Mr Arnold, who's kinda wild and kinda lost, yet deep down a really sensitive guy

who's just looking for true love, and
Ms Wiz who's kooky and romantic
and who pretends to have special, so-
called magic powers because she's so
lonely, sad and weird."

"Excuse me." Shelley had heard
enough. In spite of her nervousness,
she spoke up firmly. "The real Ms Wiz
is not like that at all. She's not lonely,
or sad and she's a lot less weird than
most of the people I have met in this
town. Her magic has made the
children in my class really happy.
She's our best friend and we love her."

Several members of the audience
started clapping, but Ted Strait stood
up angrily. "See," he shouted, pointing
at Shelley. "This child is in her evil
grip already."

For a few seconds there was uproar
in the studio until Jermaine held her
hands up for quiet. "OK, Ms Wiz.

Maybe the best way of proving your point is to show us a bit of magic right now. Why not turn this microphone into a lollipop?"

Ms Wiz shook her head and Shelley noticed that she was still staring at Brad with tears in her eyes. "I don't do spells to order," she said quietly.

"Ah, come on," said Jermaine, her voice harsher and more mocking now. "Just fly around the studio a couple of times."

Before Ms Wiz could say anything, Brad sat forward in his chair. "You see?" he said. "Our friend Ms Wiz is funny in her own way but she's no more paranormal than—" He hesitated and a sort of humming noise could be heard in the studio. A look of panic crossed his face as, to gasps from the audience, his hair rose slowly from his head and hovered in the air like a flying hedgehog.

"Brad's bald!" Someone in the
audience gasped. "He wears a wig."

"That is so not funny," Brad
screamed. As he tried to grab the
flying wig, the sound of laughter grew
in the studio.

"I think that you've proved your
point," Shelley said to Ms Wiz. "You've
showed me what Hollywood is really
like and now I want to go home."

Ms Wiz reached out her hand. "Thank you, Shelley," she called out over the din in the studio. There was a roaring sound in Shelley's ears, growing louder and louder, and suddenly everything went black.

A few seconds later, she slowly opened her eyes. She was on her sofa at home, seated between her mother and her sister Kate who were staring blankly at the TV. Like them, the screen seemed to be frozen in time.

Together, the two brightly coloured telephones rang shrilly, like an alarm clock in stereo. Mrs Kelly stirred on one side of her. Kate yawned on the other. On the TV, the couple on the *Just How Weird Is That?* show that they had been watching began shouting at one another again.

Jermaine Chance stepped between them and turned to the camera. "That's about it for today's show. Tune in tomorrow for a special programme with Brad Le Touquet and Lori Angelo. We'll be asking should they really be dabbling in magic?"

On the screen, there appeared a picture of Brad, Lori, Ms Wiz and Shelley.

"That girl looks a bit like you, Shell," said Mrs Kelly.

Ms Wiz smiled and waved at the camera, as if she knew that Shelley was watching and was now saying goodbye.

"I just love that Brad Le Touquet," said Kate. "He is such a hunk – and so nice and normal with it."

Shelley Kelly smiled to herself. "Uh-oh," she said quietly. "Fan alert."

Ms Wiz –
Millionaire

CHAPTER ONE

Chummy Lightfingers

Something rather odd was happening at St Barnabas School. It seemed to be disappearing. Bit by bit, day by day, there was less of it to see.

First a silver cup went missing from the school trophy cabinet in the hall. Then it was Miss Gomaz's cassette recorder. Then a painting from behind the headteacher's desk. Then a vacuum cleaner, three towels and 25 toilet rolls from the school store cupboard. Then the goalposts (with their nets) from the playground. Then Mr Bailey's brand-new mountain bike.

The caretaker Mr Brown started to stay late to keep guard on the school. New locks were bought. A light was set up in the playground. But nothing seemed to work.

Then, one night, the unthinkable happened. For several months, parents and teachers had been collecting money so that the school could buy a small playing-field that was for sale next door to it. Over £1,000 was being kept in a small security safe in a locked cupboard in the headteacher Mr Gilbert's office.

Until that too disappeared. When Mr Gilbert arrived at school one Monday morning, he found that the cupboard doors were open. The safe was gone.

Mr Gilbert was not a hasty man. Problems, he had found, quite often faded away if you did absolutely nothing about them.

But now everything else was fading away and it was the problem that was getting bigger. There was nothing for it. He was just going to have to take action. He lifted the phone on his desk

and rang the local police station. "PC
Boote, please," he said.

That morning, Mr Gilbert spoke to the
entire school at morning Assembly.
Behind him, sitting with the teachers,
was the unmistakable figure of PC
Boote, his peaked cap on his lap.

"Like any school, we have had our
problems," Mr Gilbert said. "Problems
in the classroom, problems in the
playground, problems with school
inspectors, problems on parents'
evenings. Problems, problems,
problems." He sighed and seemed to
drift off into a daydream.

Behind him, Mrs Hicks cleared her
throat loudly. Mr Gilbert started awake.

"Er, yes, sorry. Today we face the
biggest problem I have experienced
since arriving at St Barnabas. And I've
decided . . . What have I decided?" He

looked around helplessly. "I've decided to ask PC Boote to talk to you all." He sat down hurriedly.

The policeman walked slowly forward, put his cap on his head, and folded his arms in front of him as he looked around the hall.

"Morning, kids," he said quietly.

"Morning, PC Boote," replied the children in Assembly.

"You know, normally when I come down to see you at St Barnabas, it's to tell you about crossing the road safely – look right, left and right again – or not talking to the Danger Stranger or the importance of picking up your litter. But today I'm here to talk about something completely different." He paused dramatically. "I want to talk about nickers."

Several of the children laughed.

"By that I mean—" PC Boote seemed to be blushing "– people who are in the

habit of breaking and entering, doing a spot of half-inching and having it away on their toes before their collars can get felt. I am referring, of course, to our old friend Mr Chummy Lightfingers, your not-so-friendly local tea-leaf. Do I make myself entirely clear?"

"Er, no," someone in the front row muttered, just loud enough to hear.

"Nickers!" repeated PC Boote. "That is, people who nick things and get away with it – until now. The lads down at the station have come up with a plan – something that will catch this particular nicker red-handed." He returned to his seat and pulled out a heavy metal case from under the chair. "In this case are three security cameras which will film everything that happens at St Barnabas School, day and night." Glancing up at his audience, he clicked open the case and lifted the lid.

He looked down and stared into the

case. Then, as if not believing what he was seeing, he extended a hand and felt around inside it. Slowly, he stood up and, for a moment, seemed to be about to cry.

"All right then," he said. "Who's nicked my cameras?"

Jack Beddows and Lizzie Smith of Class Five stood gloomily outside the school hall. "I can't believe that there's someone who wants to steal things from our school," said Lizzie.

"Yeah." Jack glanced over to where PC Boote stood talking to Mr Gilbert. "And all we get is a policeman talking about nickers, Chummy Lightfingers, and then getting his own stuff stolen."

"Whoever the thief is, they must be pretty good," said Lizzie. "It's almost as if they're using magic."

The words seemed to hang in the air for a moment. Then, across the playground, a distant humming sound could be heard.

A black van, with the words *Wizard Security Agency* written in gold letters on the side, drew up outside the school gates. A woman in a trim, dark suit stepped out, pushed open the school gate and walked briskly across the playground.

"Is that who I think it is?" said Jack.

"And, if it is, why is she dressed like a businesswoman?" asked Lizzie.

Without a moment's hesitation, the woman approached Mr Gilbert and PC Boote.

"Can I help you?" asked Mr Gilbert impatiently.

"The name's Wiz – Ms Wiz . . . private detective."

Jack and Lizzie smiled at one another.

"Wiz?" Mr Gilbert looked nervous. He had a few memories of Ms Wiz. Whenever she appeared at the school, things became even more difficult than they were usually. "I thought you had, er, retired."

"So did I," said Ms Wiz. "But life's been a bit quiet recently. And now there have been so many burglaries in the town that I decided that a bit of magic was needed. So I've gone into the crime-busting game."

"A crime-buster with black nail-varnish? I don't think so," chuckled PC Boote. "Leave it to the experts, lady."

"This police officer is absolutely right," said Mr Gilbert. "Magic's for kids. This is a problem for grown-ups." He looked up to see Jack and Lizzie casually standing nearby. "Jack, Lizzie. Please escort this visitor off the school premises," he said.

Jack and Lizzie followed Ms Wiz back to her van. "It's so unfair," said Lizzie.

"And stupid," said Ms Wiz. "Because it just so happens that I know the identity of the thief."

"How?" asked Jack.

Ms Wiz smiled knowingly. "I have my methods," she said, and reaching into the top pocket of her jacket, she took out a small, white plastic card and handed it to Jack. "This is what I call 'the Magic Revealer'. Hold it very still on the palm of your hand and you will see a photograph of your thief at work."

Jack looked down. "Er, it's blank," he said.

But, as Lizzie peered over his shoulder, a hint of colour began to appear on the white of the card. As the picture grew clearer, a small figure could be seen. It was taking a small security safe from the cupboard in Mr Gilbert's office.

Jack gasped. "It's Kevin Lightly," he said. "He's only just started school. He's in Class One with Mrs Hicks."

"I can't believe it," whispered Lizzie. "He's such a funny, shy little boy."

"He must be working for someone else," said Jack. "We can't report him to the police."

"Maybe we could just . . . talk to him," said Lizzie.

Ms Wiz took back the Magic Revealer and slipped it into her pocket. "My thoughts exactly," she said.

CHAPTER TWO

A Family Business

It was an evening like any other for the Lightly family. Dodgy Dave Lightly was on the sofa studying the instruction manual for some stolen security cameras. Across the room, his wife Anita the Cheater was sitting at a machine that printed fake £50 notes. And, on the floor, sat their only son Kevin, doing some homework his father had given him – practising how to open padlocks with a pin.

Dodgy Dave looked around him and smiled. "My little family," he said. "Other people might go out to the cinema or sit in front of the TV but the Lightlys make our own entertainment in the old-fashioned way – working at the family business." He sniffed, suddenly feeling rather emotional. "Makes you feel proud, don't it?"

Kevin looked up. "But why can't we do some other kind of work, Dad? When people ask me what you do, why do I always have to tell them you're in the removal business?"

"But it's true, love," said Anita. "Your dad does remove things – and very well too."

"I'm like Robin Hood," said Dodgy Dave. "I steal from the rich – that's everyone else – and give to the poor – that's us."

"Except nobody from St Barnabas is very rich," muttered Kevin.

"Don't be rude to your father," murmured Anita. "You're very lucky he spends time helping you learn a trade. You'll thank him when you grow up."

"But I don't want to be a thief," said Kevin. "I want to be a teacher."

Dodgy Dave and Anita the Cheater stared at their son in amazement. "Any more of that talk and I'll send you to your room," Dave said eventually. "You'll break your poor mother's heart, you will."

Just then, the doorbell rang. "Now who could that be?" said Dodgy Dave, casually throwing a blanket over the stolen goods on the sofa.

"Maybe it's the police," said Kevin nervously.

"Nah, they don't bother ringing – they just kick the door down," said Anita.

Dodgy Dave stood by the door. "Who is it, please?" he called out in his politest voice.

"The name's Wiz – Ms Wiz . . . neighbourhood advice officer," came the voice from outside. "I'm looking for the Lightly family."

"They moved a couple of months

ago," said Dodgy Dave, winking at Anita. "I heard they emigrated to Australia."

There was a moment's pause. Then, as a faint humming noise could be heard from outside, the lock on the door drew back and the door slowly opened. "Thank you so much," said Ms Wiz, entering the room.

"Hey, that was good," said Dodgy Dave, running his finger down the side of the door. "Are you in the breaking and entering business too?"

Without a word, Ms Wiz reached into her top pocket for the Magic Revealer. "My card," she said.

Dodgy Dave looked down at the card in his hand. "It's blank," he said. "Hang on, it's one of those joke cards. There's a picture of someone coming up." He squinted at it more closely. "It looks a bit like our Kevin."

"It is Kevin," said Ms Wiz. "And

he's carrying the safe at St Barnabas."

Anita peered over her husband's shoulder. "Ah, look at him, the little mite," she said.

"Have you got another one of these?" asked Dodgy Dave. "Maybe we could get it framed."

Ms Wiz frowned. "Aren't you worried that your son has been photographed stealing a safe from his school?" she said.

"Kevin?" Dodgy Dave winked at his wife. "You can't prove nothing. He was with us all that evening, whichever evening it was."

"That's right," said Anita. "It must have been the night his dear old grandma was here. We've got loads of witnesses."

"As it happens," said Ms Wiz. "I have decided not to hand this evidence over to the police. I wanted to come round here to talk to you about giving up all this thieving."

Anita looked puzzled. "Why would we want to do that, then?" she asked.

"Because it's wrong," said Ms Wiz firmly. "And because, if you go on doing it, you're all going to end up in jail."

"And because I don't like it," murmured Kevin under his breath.

"But—" Ms Wiz smiled. "I want to give you another chance. I believe that, given an opportunity in life, all of us are basically good."

"That's true enough," said Dodgy Dave. "I'm good at breaking and entering. Anita here's an artist when it comes to faking notes and Kevin's got lovely little fingers for opening locks—"

"Let me put it another way." Ms Wiz spoke more sharply. "I am a private paranormal detective. I have my methods. Because I have rather special, magical powers, I can produce evidence that other detectives can only dream of.

For example—" She reached into the leather bag at her feet, and took out a matchbox. "What would you say this is, Kevin?" She carefully opened the box.

"Ugh," said Kevin. "It seems to be a dead fly."

"Actually, it's a camera," said Ms Wiz. "I call this my 'Magic Visualiser'. I released it outside St Barnabas School. It followed you into the school when you broke in and photographed everything

you did. The result appears on the Magic Revealer. You see, with my paranormal powers, I can make things move, disappear—"

"We can all do that," said Dodgy Dave.

"I can even predict what's going to happen in the future." Ms Wiz took what seemed to be a small photograph frame out of her bag. "This is my Magic Predictor," she said. "It's like a video recorder, only it can film things which have yet to happen."

Dodgy Dave examined the frame thoughtfully. "That could be handy," he murmured.

"But if you promise to give up thieving, I won't hand over any of this evidence to PC Boote."

"Could you just show me how the Magic Predictor works?" Dodgy Dave wandered casually over to the television and switched it on. "For instance, could you predict what would be on this TV channel on Saturday evening at, say, eight o'clock?"

A faint humming sound filled the room and a small cloud of fog enveloped the Magic Predictor. When it cleared, a picture could be seen in the frame. "There you are," said Ms Wiz. "It seems to be some sort of game show. There are lots of little balls with numbers on them."

"Oh yes, so it is." Dodgy Dave picked up a pen and, staring at the frame, jotted something down on the back of his hand. "Thank you, Ms Wiz," he said, switching the television off. "You've really made me think about things." He stood up. "I've decided. I'm through with nicking things. We're all definitely going straight from now on."

"We are?" said Anita.

"Excellent," said Ms Wiz, returning the Magic Predictor to her bag. "I knew that, if we discussed all this in a civilised way, you'd see sense."

"And, goodness me, you were right," said Dodgy Dave. "You've certainly changed our lives, Ms Wiz. We'll return the stuff we took from St Barnabas during half-term."

"We will?" said Anita.

Dodgy Dave walked quickly to the door. "Thanks a bunch, then," he said.

"You're very welcome." Ms Wiz smiled. "Goodbye, Kevin. Goodbye, Mr and Mrs Lightly."

Nodding and smiling, Dodgy Dave closed the door behind Ms Wiz. He walked slowly back into the room. "She has changed our life an' all," he said, staring thoughtfully at the back of his hand.

"That Predictor thing was showing the National Lottery," said Kevin.

"That's right, son. And now I know the winning numbers."

"Oh, Dave." A smile came to Anita's

face. "You're a genius."

"All we need to do is buy a ticket for Saturday and we'll be made for life," chuckled Dodgy Dave. Soon Mr and Mrs Lightly were dancing around the room. "We're rich! We're rich!" they shouted.

From below the window, Ms Wiz heard the sounds of laughter. She looked up and smiled. "Another job well done," she said quietly.

CHAPTER THREE

The Fickle Finger of Fate

The following Monday, there were strange scenes outside St Barnabas School. Photographers lined the street, newspaper reporters with notebooks and tape recorders jostled at the gate to the playground where PC Boote was trying to keep order.

Everybody wanted to catch a glimpse of the winners of that weekend's fifteen million pound triple roll-over lottery, the Lightly family. The winners, Mr and Mrs Lightly, had not been seen in public but the rumour had spread that, on Monday morning, they would be taking their little boy Kevin to school as usual.

A surge of bodies towards the corner of the street was the first sign that the Lightlys were approaching. When they

appeared, a crowd gathered round.
Over the click and clatter of cameras,
reporters shouted their questions.

"How are you feeling, Dave?"

"Which of you chose the lucky
numbers?"

"What are you going to do with the
money, Anita?"

"Give us a wave, Kevin!"

"Hold up, hold up." Dave Lightly
raised both hands for silence. "At the end
of the day, to be fair, it hasn't quite sunk
in yet," he said. "But, as you can see,
we're just an ordinary family taking our
little lad to school. Just because I
happen to have fifteen million quid in
the bank, that doesn't change anything."

PC Boote pushed his way through the
crowd. "Dodgy Dave Lightly, a
millionaire – I've seen everything now,"
he murmured as he led the family
towards the school gates.

Dodgy Dave smiled coldly. "It'll be

Mr Lightly from now on, thank you, Constable."

As Kevin Lightly entered the playground, he was immediately surrounded by children from Class One, laughing and congratulating him and asking him questions.

Jack and Lizzie paused to watch the scene.

"One day Ms Wiz pays a visit to the Lightly family. The following weekend, they win the lottery," Lizzie murmured.

"It could be a coincidence," said Jack.

They watched Kevin as he pushed through the crowd. As he passed them, he glanced in their direction, then looked away quickly.

"Something weird's going on here," said Lizzie. "I think we need to speak to that paranormal detective, don't you?"

*

But it was Ms Wiz who found them. That afternoon, as Jack and Lizzie were walking home after school, an extremely unusual sight awaited them on the High Street. A long, white limousine was parked outside the chemist, the newsagent, the fish and chip shop, and the pub. Several people stood on the pavement nearby, admiring the car and peering through its darkened windows to see who was inside.

As Jack and Lizzie passed, the limo seemed to purr into life. After a few moments, it moved forward at walking pace, staying a few metres behind them.

"Don't look now," murmured Lizzie. "But I think we're being followed by a giant car."

One of the car's windows opened slightly. "Want a lift, then?" said a woman's voice.

Lizzie glanced in the direction of the car. A hand was now beckoning through the window. Lizzie couldn't help noticing that on its fingers was black nail-varnish.

The car stopped and the third of three back doors opened to reveal, lounging on the back seat, the elegant figure of a woman in a blue silk dress. "The name's Wiz – Ms Wiz . . . millionaire," she said.

"What's going on, Ms Wiz?" asked Jack. "Where did you get this flash motor?"

"This is not so much a flash motor as a moving luxury home," said Ms Wiz.

When they stepped into the car, it was like entering a rather grand sitting-room. There were low lights all round. Soft music was playing in the background. In one corner, beside a large leather chair, was a table on which there were crisps and nuts and bottles of lemonade, while in another corner there was a TV.

Ms Wiz waved a hand in the direction of the table. "Help yourself to anything you like," she said.

"Hey, great spell, Ms Wiz," said Jack, settling into one of the chairs.

"It is rather magical, isn't it?" said Ms Wiz. "But it's not a spell. Kevin's dad, that dear Mr Lightly, gave me a few pounds – well, a couple of million pounds to be precise – to thank me, and I thought I'd give myself a treat. I don't like champagne. I can't stand shopping. But I just love cars. So I got the very biggest one I could find and hired myself a chauffeur." She lifted the receiver of a white telephone from the wall beside her. "We'll just drive around for a while. Yes—" Ms Wiz's smile became a little forced. "I know that's what we've been doing all day but we're going to do it a bit more."

"What exactly was Kevin's dad thanking you for?" asked Lizzie.

"For saving him from a life of crime. I went to the Lightlys' flat, talked to them about what a good thing honesty was and he said, 'Fine, OK, Ms Wiz.' And that was that."

"And three days later, he won the lottery," said Lizzie.

"Yes." Ms Wiz laughed. "The fickle finger of fate. Isn't it marvellous? By the way, what exactly is a lottery?"

Jack and Lizzie glanced at one another. "It's where lots of people buy a ticket with six numbers and the winning numbers are announced on a TV show every week."

"On TV." Ms Wiz looked thoughtful. "Would that be on a Saturday night?"

"That's the main one," said Lizzie.

"So if someone had a Magic Predictor, which told the future, they might be able to—"

"Oh, Ms Wiz," groaned Jack. "What have you done?"

"Could we see this Magic Predictor?" asked Lizzie.

"Bit of a problem there," said Ms Wiz quietly. "The old magic doesn't seem to be working quite so well this week. In fact, it's not working at all."

There was a brief silence in the car. "What about the spells?" said Jack. "The FISH powder? The Mickey Mouse alarm clock/time machine." A sudden thought occurred to him. "What about Herbert, the magic rat?"

"Oh, he's fine." Ms Wiz reached into the sleeve of her dress and carefully took out a brown and white rat. "Only he can't talk any more. He's – well, he's just a normal rat."

"Normal? Herbert? I don't believe it," said Lizzie.

Ms Wiz shrugged and looked away. "Who needs magic when you've got

loads of money?"

"D'you remember the first time you came to St Barnabas?" Jack asked suddenly. "You told us that magic should never be used for personal greed. Now Kevin's dad has won the lottery thanks to your magic and you're driving around in a big car – that's why your spells don't work any more."

"You win some, you lose some." Ms Wiz laughed nervously. "Thank goodness that, although I now have a huge fortune, I'm just the same old me."

Jack and Lizzie looked more closely at Ms Wiz. She seemed to have done something fluffy and expensive to her hair and was definitely wearing more make-up than she ever used to. There was a strange, empty look to her green eyes.

"Yes," said Jack uncertainly. "Thank goodness for that."

"What about the Lightlys?" asked Lizzie. "Have they changed?"

"Only for the better," said Ms Wiz. "David has told me that he's going to give lots of money to good causes. They live on the top floor of the Grand Hotel now. In fact, I'm going round for tea tomorrow. David said that we millionaires should stick together. Maybe you'd like to see them too."

Jack glanced at Lizzie. "I think that would be an excellent idea," he said.

CHAPTER FOUR

The Same, Only Much Richer

When the lift opened on the top floor of the Grand Hotel the next day, Ms Wiz, Jack and Lizzie found that a butler was waiting for them. He seemed to be swaying slightly.

"Would you be Mish—" He closed his eyes and shook his head. "Mishter Lightly's tea guests?" he asked in a low, slurred voice.

"That's us," said Ms Wiz brightly.

"Step this way, please." The butler turned and walked slowly down the corridor, occasionally bouncing off the walls.

"I think he must be drunk," whispered Lizzie.

"Nonsense," said Ms Wiz. "That's

probably just the way he walks."

At the end of the corridor was a pair of large double doors. Holding on to the two golden door-handles and resting his head against the door, the butler intoned, "And who shall I shay ish calling?"

"We are Ms Dolores Wisdom, Mr Jack Beddows and Miss Elizabeth Smith," said Ms Wiz in her poshest voice.

The butler leant forward and opened the door, losing his balance briefly. He took a deep breath and announced, "Ms Jack Wizzo, Mr Brenda Toes and Elish . . . Elish Whatshername." Then he stepped aside with a low bow and, in this position, backed out of the door behind them.

Ms Wiz, Jack and Lizzie were in a big, high-ceilinged room. Through a haze of cigar smoke, four men could be seen sitting at a table in the middle of the room, playing cards.

One of the men looked in their direction. "Well, if it isn't good old Ms Wiz," he said. "Come to join the party, then?"

"Hello, David," said Ms Wiz with a polite, strained smile. "You invited me to tea. I took the liberty of bringing along Jack and Lizzie from Kevin's school."

"Tea? You're having a laugh!" Dave's voice echoed around the room. "Nobody drinks tea round here. It's champagne all the way."

Ms Wiz glanced at the floor which was strewn with empty bottles. "So I see," she said.

"Want to join us, then? The kids can go and see Kevin – he's just down the corridor, playing with his new, *stonkingly* expensive computer."

"I'm not a gambler myself." Ms Wiz walked slowly towards the table. "So this is what you do all day since you won the lottery. You haven't helped any good causes at all."

"Course I have." Dodgy Dave chuckled. "I'm buying a football club. I'm looking very seriously at a tropical island in the Pacific. I'm giving my mates a good time, aren't I, lads?"

"Diamond geezer, old Dave," said one of the men. "Yeah, heart of gold," said another. The third seemed to have fallen asleep, his head on the table.

"Then there's my family." Dodgy Dave stood up and walked towards a side door. "They're another good cause." He opened the door. Anita Lightly was reclining on a giant bed in a pink silk dressing-gown. A young man was manicuring her toenails while she thumbed through a catalogue, a pen in her hand. "Once she used to work all day at her printing business. Now she can do all her shopping without getting out of bed. That's a good cause in anyone's language."

He closed the door and walked down
a corridor to another side-room. Ms
Wiz, Jack and Lizzie looked through the
door to see three of the children from
Class One in front of a giant computer
screen. Kevin Lightly stood behind
them, watching as they played. "Ever
since he got that computer, he's the
most popular kid in his class," said
Dodgy Dave. At that moment, Kevin
looked up and waved, unsmilingly.

"He doesn't seem to be having much fun himself," said Lizzie.

Dodgy Dave shrugged. "He's gone a bit quiet ever since we became millionaires. I expect it's the excitement."

"But when you were talking to those reporters, you said you were just an ordinary family and that being a multimillionaire wasn't going to change you," said Jack.

"It hasn't," said Dodgy Dave cheerfully. "We're just the same, only much, much richer. We've got ourselves a new hobby – spending loads of money."

Ms Wiz put her arm round Dodgy Dave's shoulders. "David," she said in a quiet, dangerous voice. "Do you remember when we first met I told you that I was a paranormal detective?"

Dodgy Dave nodded.

"Well, my special, paranormal powers

are telling me that you have used my magic to win the lottery." She stood back and raised both her hands. "And what magic can give, magic can take away."

At that moment, a faint humming noise could be heard in the room. As it grew louder, Ms Wiz closed her eyes, and clenched her fists. "Please. *Please*," she whispered. But, after a few seconds her shoulders slumped and the sound faded. For a moment, there was silence in the room.

"Who *is* this nutter?" said one of the men sitting at the table.

Ms Wiz looked around the room. "Gone," she whispered. "The magic's gone." Then, with a little sob, she ran to the double doors.

When Jack and Lizzie found her, she was standing by the lift, her face buried in her hands.

"Are you all right, Ms Wiz?" Lizzie placed a hand on her shoulder.

"It's all over. I've lost my powers."
Ms Wiz looked up and there were tears
in her eyes. "What am I going to do?"

The following day, Jack Beddows
arrived at St Barnabas School with a
plan. It wasn't a great plan. It was a plan
that could very easily go horribly
wrong. But he and Lizzie had agreed
that it was the only plan they could

think of which had a chance of bringing magic back into the life of Ms Wiz.

For the plan to have any chance of success, they needed the help of Kevin Lightly.

At first, when Jack and Lizzie explained what he would have to do, Kevin was reluctant. Then Jack and Lizzie told him of some of their magical adventures with Ms Wiz in the past – about travelling back in time and rescuing Jack, about saving Podge from becoming a zombie slave in the underworld, about Archimedes the mathematical barn owl and Herbert the magic rat.

"That Magic Visualiser of hers was pretty good," Kevin looked thoughtful. "And the Magic Predictor was amazing."

"But unless we do something, there will be no more spells because the golden rule about magic is that it must

never be used for selfish purposes,"
said Jack.

"Ms Wiz has said she's going to give
everything away, even her car," said
Lizzie. "But while your dad's still a
millionaire, she's helpless."

Kevin looked at them in
astonishment. "You want us to give all
our money away?"

"It's not as if it has made you any
happier," said Lizzie.

"Even Mum says she's bored of lying
around all day," Kevin said quietly. "It'll
be good if life could go back to the way
it was, but with Dad and Mum doing
normal jobs. But how would we do it?"

"All we need is a bit of inside
information." Jack smiled. "And you
can leave the rest to us."

CHAPTER FIVE

The Magic Truth-Teller

Mr Gilbert was in an excellent mood. Thanks to his talk to the school, all the stolen property (except for a few toilet rolls) had been returned during half-term. And now, it looked as if St Barnabas was going to be able to buy the playing-field next door.

He sat at his desk, remembering how Jack Beddows and Lizzie Smith of Class Five had told him that Mr Lightly was interested in giving the final £10,000 to the school on the condition that there would be a big presentation to mark the handing over of the money.

He had invited parents, some local reporters, even PC Boote to today's Assembly. He had even agreed to Jack's suggestion that Ms Wiz would put on a magic show for the children of the school.

He stood up and rubbed his hands. Mrs Gilbert would be proud of the way he had sorted out the school's problems. It was time for Assembly.

"Today is a very special day for St Barnabas School." Mr Gilbert stood before the entire school, then smiled at his guests of honour who were sitting in the front row.

"It's special," the headteacher continued, "because, at long last, the school will be able to have its own playing-field, thanks to a magnificent gesture by our most famous parents, Mr and Mrs Lightly."

To deafening applause, Dodgy Dave and Anita stood up. "Too kind, too kind," said Anita, curtseying one way then the other. "You're very welcome," said Dodgy Dave, a large cigar clamped between his teeth.

As the clapping died down, Dodgy Dave picked up the suitcase that was under his chair and stepped forward. "I thought of giving the school a cheque for the money but in the end I thought you'd like to see some real money." He opened the case to reveal that it was neatly packed with crisp £50 notes.

"Goodness, look how new these notes are," said Mr Gilbert. "It's as if they've just been printed."

"Eh?" A look of alarm crossed Dodgy Dave's face. "Er, yes, I collected them from the bank this morning."

"Perhaps you'd like to give a little message of inspiration to the children," said the headteacher.

Dodgy Dave thought for a moment, then took a step forward. "Kids," he said solemnly. "I want you all to know

that, at the end of the day, to be fair, money isn't everything. What matters in this world is not money itself – but what money can buy you. Big cars, for instance. Houses with jacuzzis on every floor. Mink fur coats for the wife. Holidays in very sunny places. And above all—" He hesitated and seemed to be overcome with emotion. "Quality time, every day of the week, to play cards with your best mates."

As Dodgy Dave swaggered back to his seat, Mr Gilbert seemed briefly to be lost for words. "Er, thank you, Mr Lightly, for those thoughts," he said. "And to mark the occasion, at the special request of Class Five, we have invited the one and only Ms Wiz to show us some of her famous magic spells."

Dodgy Dave leant over to Anita. "I thought that woman's magic didn't work any more," he murmured.

To cheers from the children, Ms Wiz

appeared from behind a curtain. In her hand, she held a small plastic wand. "Behold a special wand which I call 'the Magic Truth-Teller'," she said.

"Oh yeah?" Anita giggled. "I saw those wands being sold down the market yesterday."

"The Magic Truth-Teller has the power to tell what is real from what is false. Only if something is not entirely genuine will the red light at the end light up."

She advanced on the front row and touched Anita's fur coat. Nothing happened to the wand. "That's real fur," said Ms Wiz.

"Shame," said Katrina rather loudly from the back.

Ms Wiz touched the ring on Anita's finger. Again, the wand remained the same. "Congratulations," said Ms Wiz. "That's a real diamond."

"What d'you expect?" muttered

Dodgy Dave.

Ms Wiz walked back to the front of the Assembly. As if noticing the case full of money for the first time, she clicked it open and, before Dodgy Dave could stop her, laid the wand on the notes inside. The red light lit up immediately. "Oh dear," said Ms Wiz. "The Magic Truth-Teller is revealing that there's something not quite right about these notes."

"Hello hello hello." PC Boote sat forward, suddenly interested.

"It's a bloomin' wind-up." Dodgy Dave laughed nervously. "She's pressing a button on the wand. She's the one that's fake."

But Ms Wiz had produced a picture-frame from her bag. "This looks like a normal frame, doesn't it? In fact, it's a Magic Predictor." She smiled down at the front row. "Isn't it, David?"

"I've warned you," said Dodgy Dave

between his teeth.

"It can reveal the future, of course –
but it can also reveal the past." Ms Wiz
put the frame on a table. "Let's look at
some scenes from the past of our special
guests," she said. "Shall we say, the
evening they decided to buy their
winning lottery ticket. Or the night last
September when there was a break-in
at the post office on the High Street."

"How did she know about that?"

Dodgy Dave whispered to Anita.

"But first of all we're going to see Mrs Lightly at work on her special printing machine."

There was a scream from Anita. "Stop her, Dave," she shouted.

Dodgy Dave stepped forward and put an arm round Ms Wiz's shoulders. "Great magic show, Ms Wiz," he said loudly, then whispered in her ear, "Are you mad? What are you trying to do to me?"

"Give all your money to charity and

I'll stop now," said Ms Wiz in a low voice.

A moan of despair came from Dodgy Dave. "How about half?" he murmured through the side of his mouth.

Ms Wiz shrugged herself free. "On with the show," she said.

"No!" He turned to the audience, a desperate, fixed grin on his face. "I've just made a very big decision, ladies and gentlemen," he said in a strangled voice. "I'm through with money. I'm going to give it all away."

There was a gasp from around the hall. "Dodgy Dave giving away money?" muttered PC Boote. "Something very funny's going on here."

"It's only cash, after all." With a trembling hand, Dodgy Dave took out a chequebook, wrote on it and gave it to Ms Wiz. "Here's a blank cheque made out to the school," he said. "You can do what you like with it." He snapped the suitcase shut. "Come on, love, let's go home." Grabbing Anita by the hand, he scurried out of the hall.

For a moment, there was silence. Smiling, Ms Wiz gave the cheque to Mr Gilbert. "A donation to good causes," she said. "And I can't think of a better cause than a playing-field for the children of St Barnabas."

Cheers echoed around the hall.

"Well," Mr Gilbert stared nervously at the cheque, "I said today would be special and I think it was. Er, wasn't it?"

After the Assembly had dispersed, Jack and Lizzie found Ms Wiz in the playground, talking to Kevin Lightly.

"Great magic show, Ms Wiz," said Jack.

Ms Wiz smiled at Kevin. "It's amazing what a plastic wand, an old picture frame and a bit of inside information can do," she said.

"Will Mum and Dad go back to nicking things like they used to?" Kevin asked.

"Not now that they know the power of magic," said Ms Wiz.

"That's all very well," said Lizzie. "But what about your own magic?"

Ms Wiz was about to reply when a familiar voice came from her bag. "Golly gosh and jimminy." Herbert the rat peered out. "I've just had the most

awful dream. I was a normal rat. The *embarrassment*, my dear."

"Don't think about it, Herbert," said Ms Wiz, turning towards the gate.

"Excuse me, miss." They turned to see the figure of PC Boote approaching. "Do you happen to be in possession of information about Mr and Mrs Lightly which could be of assistance to the police?" he asked.

Ms Wiz glanced at Kevin. "Only that they've generously given all their money to good causes," she said.

"Hmm." PC Boote looked unconvinced. "If I were you, I'd stick to magic and leave the crime-busting to the experts," he said, putting away his notebook.

Ms Wiz smiled. "I think that's the best advice I've had in a long time," she said.